THOMAS & FRIE[NDS]

Travel with Thomas

Illustrated by Tino Santanach

A GOLDEN BOOK · NEW YORK

Thomas the Tank Engine & Friends™

CREATED BY BRITT ALLCROFT

Based on The Railway Series by The Reverend W Awdry.
© 2004, 2007 Gullane (Thomas) LLC.
Thomas the Tank Engine & Friends and Thomas & Friends are trademarks of Gullane (Thomas) Limited.
Thomas the Tank Engine & Friends & Design is Reg. U.S. Pat. & Tm. Off.
HIT and the HIT Entertainment logo are trademarks of HIT Entertainment Limited.
All rights reserved. Published in the United States by Golden Books, an imprint of
Random House Children's Books, a division of Random House, Inc., New York, and in Canada by
Random House of Canada Limited, Toronto. Golden Books, A Golden Book, and the G colophon are registered trademarks of Random House, Inc.
Parts of this book were originally published in slightly different form as *All Aboard!* and *One-Stop Color and Match* by Golden Books in 2004.
ISBN: 978-0-375-83953-5
www.randomhouse.com/kids/thomas
www.thomasandfriends.com
Printed in the United States of America
24 23 22 21 20 19 18 17 16 15 14

HiT entertainment

Cranky unloads a box marked "URGENT."
The box is for Sir Topham Hatt.

"If it says 'urgent,' it must be important!" says Thomas. "I'll take it to Sir Topham Hatt right away!"

What do you think is in the box?
Draw it here!

Gordon pulls up to the station.

"An urgent package needs a speedy train!"
says Gordon. "So I'll take it!"

Thomas is left behind.
"I'm a speedy train, too," peeps Thomas.

Gordon tries to take a shortcut but finds out that there are rocks blocking the tracks!

"*Help!* I have an urgent package for Sir Topham Hatt," says Gordon. "But I'm stuck!" "I'll take it down the hill for you," says Toby.

Toby clickity-clacks quickly down the hill.

Help Toby get to the bottom of the hill, where Percy is waiting.

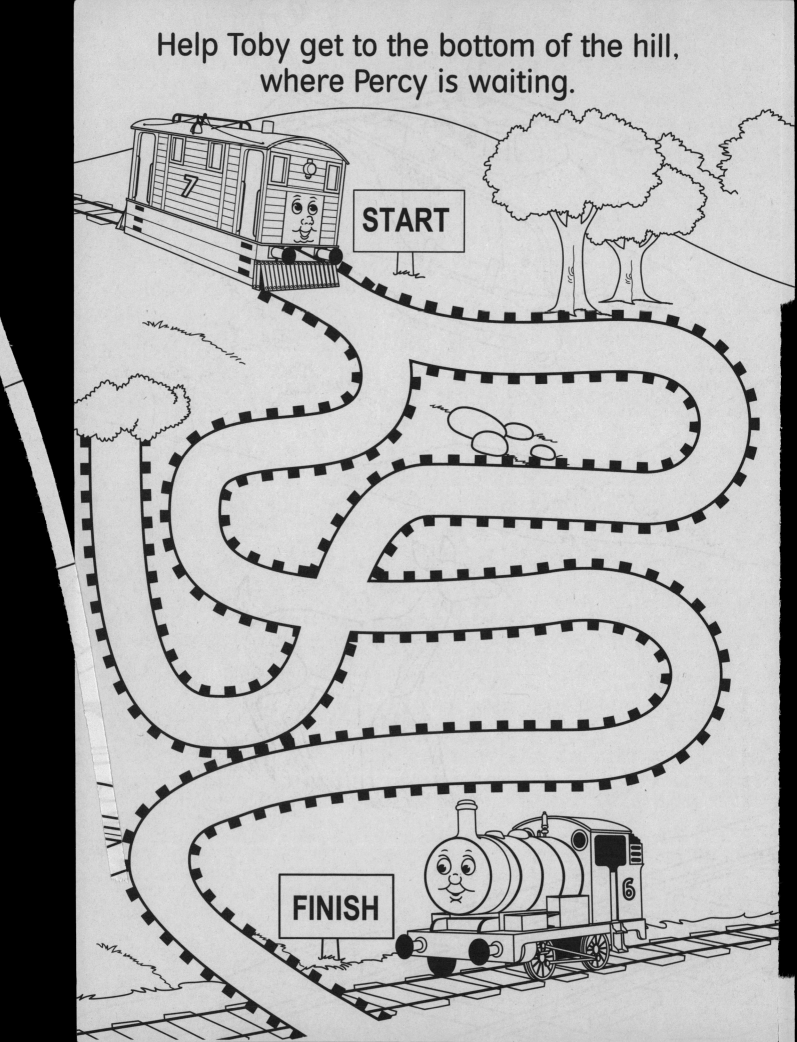

"Thank you for bringing the urgent package down," says Percy. "Now I can take it!"

"Sir Topham Hatt will be very proud
of me," Percy toots.

Two of these pictures of Percy are the same. Circle them!

A

B

C

D

E

Answer: A and C.

Percy meets James, who is pulling a Troublesome Truck. "I won't release my brakes until you give the package to James," says the Troublesome Truck.

Percy is cross, but he knows the delivery has to get to Sir Topham Hatt fast, so he gives it to him.

James is happy that he will now be the one
to deliver the urgent package.

James is going so fast, he almost doesn't see the broken track.

"Oh, no!" says James. "How will I get the urgent package to Sir Topham Hatt?"

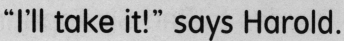

"I'll take it!" says Harold.

Harold hurries to find Sir Topham Hatt.

Harold sees Thomas far below. He was faster than Gordon after all!

"Where's my package?"
asks Sir Topham Hatt.

Look at this picture and the one on the facing page. Find eight things that are different.

Answers: On this page,
• the buttons on his shoe are missing
• a line has been removed from one shoe
• he is showing his fingers on both hands
• his jacket collar is missing
• there are fewer buttons on his vest
• his tie is missing
• he is smiling
• his ear looks different

"I have it, sir!" says Harold. Then he tells Sir Topham Hatt and Thomas the long story about the package.

URGENT

Sir Topham Hatt opens the urgent delivery.

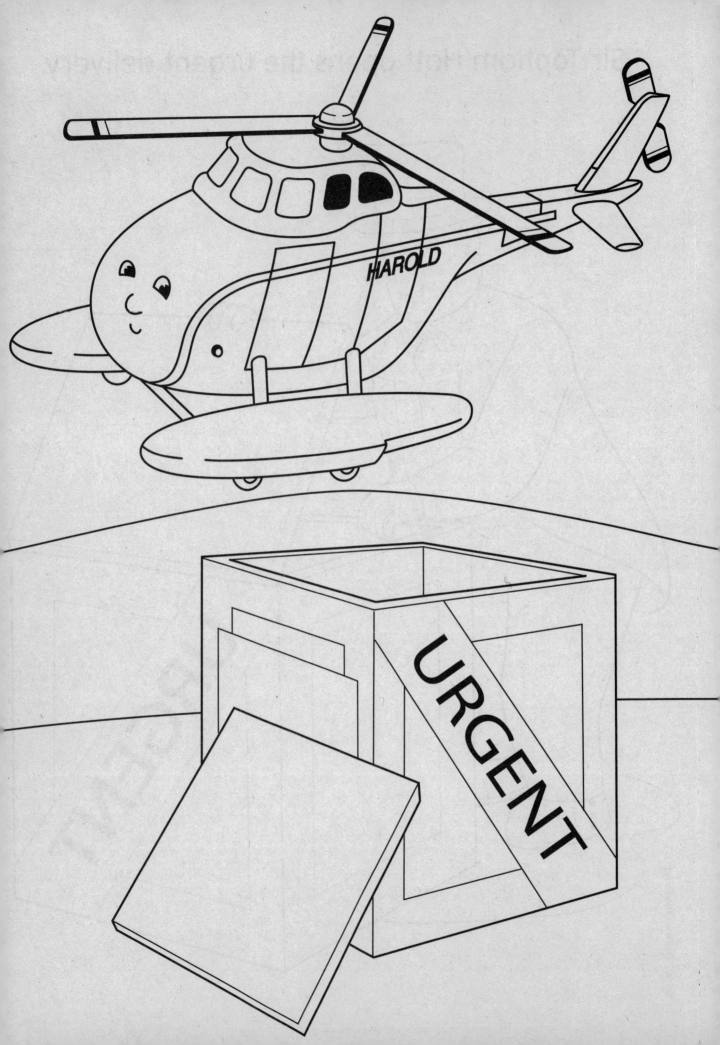

It's a shiny new hat!
"Just in time for tonight's big party!" says
Sir Topham Hatt.

"And, Thomas, next time there is an urgent delivery," says Sir Topham Hatt, "I want *you* to bring it!"

Thomas peeps proudly . . .

. . . and heads to the engine shed with
a smile on his face.

THOMAS & FRIENDS™

All Aboard!

Illustrated by Red Giraffe

Thomas and his friends are always ready
to work hard around the Island of Sodor.

James' paint shines in the rising sun.

Percy is cheerful and makes work fun
for everyone.

His favorite job is pulling the mail train.

Edward is kind to small and big engines.

Henry and his driver make a good team.

Find 5 differences between these 2 pages.

Answers: On this page,
Henry does not have a smoke puff; the flowers are missing; Edward and Henry
have empty tenders; Henry is looking at Edward;
a cloud is missing.

Gordon thinks he has the most important job on the Island of Sodor.

He pulls the Express into the station.

Toby and Mavis work together
at the quarry.

Ben and Bill are twin engines.

They work in the clay pits.

Bulstrode delivers a full load of materials to the docks.

Cranky lifts the crates to load freight cars.

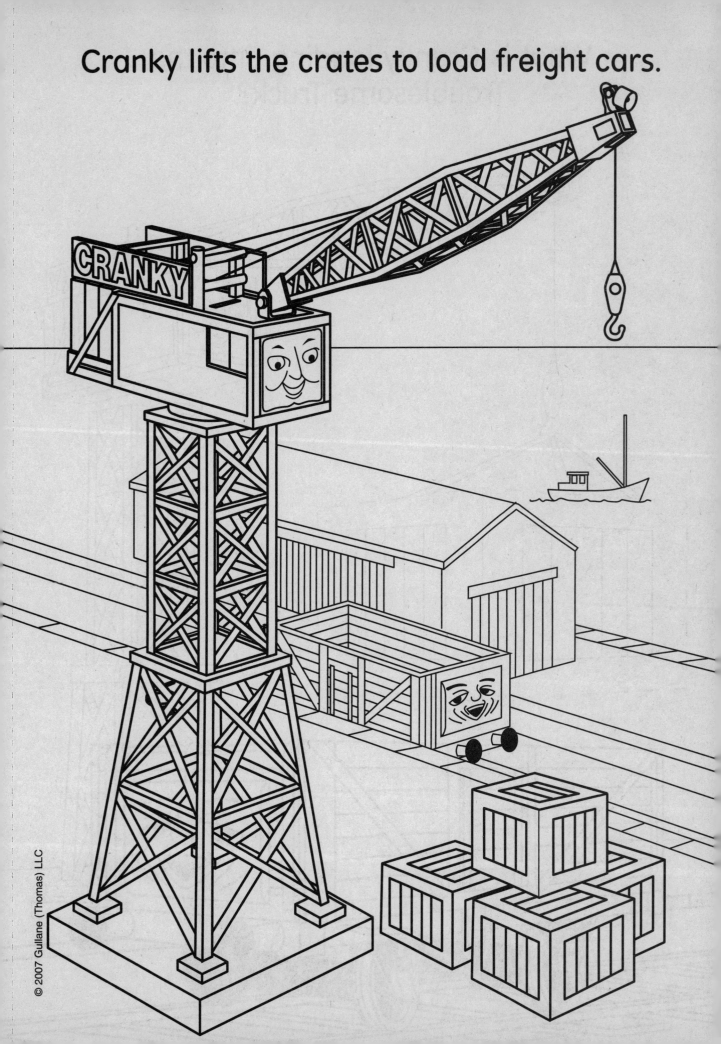

What is Cranky loading onto the Troublesome Truck?

Circle the things that Troublesome Trucks might carry.

A

B

C

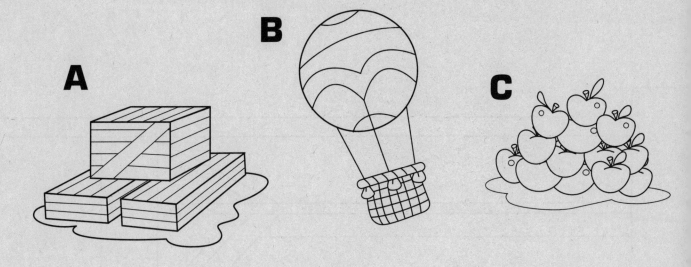

D

E

Answers: A, C, and D.

Salty always has a tale to tell while getting the day's work done.

No job is too big for Harvey!
He lifts heavy loads at the docks.

Donald and Douglas do twice the work . . .

. . . and have twice the fun!

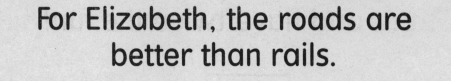

For Elizabeth, the roads are
better than rails.

Which path will lead Elizabeth straight to the Yard?

Here's Bertie! He's ready for a friendly race with Thomas.

Follow the lines to see who wins the race to the station.

Answer: Thomas.

Harold watches over everyone in the Yard.

His engine friends are always happy
to look up and see him.

Draw a line to match each friend to his home.

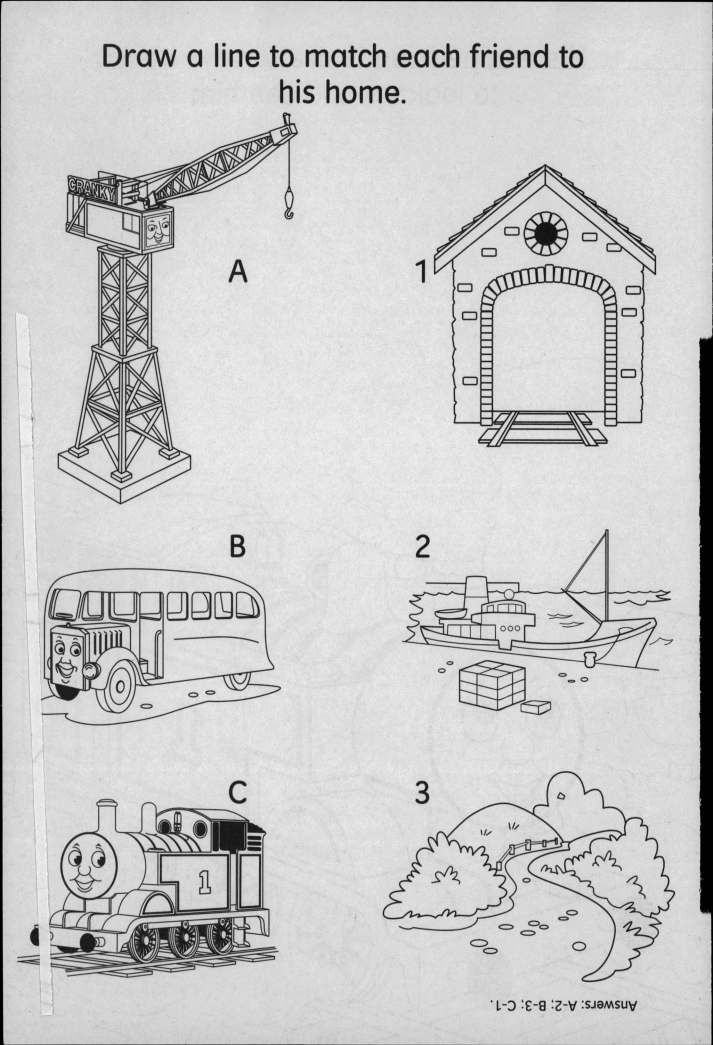

A

1

B

2

C

3

"Right on time, Thomas!" cheers Sir Topham Hatt. "You're a Really Useful Engine."

Thanks to Thomas and his friends, another day of work is done.

THOMAS & FRIENDS™

One-Stop Color and Match

Illustrated by Tino Santanach

Spring is just around the corner.

Sir Topham Hatt is wearing his new spring suit.

The Most Beautiful Station contest
happens every spring.

Sir Topham Hatt needs every engine's help to get ready for it.

MOST BEAUTIFUL STATION CONTEST

© 2007 Gullane (Thomas) LLC

What can be used to clean up the station at Maron?

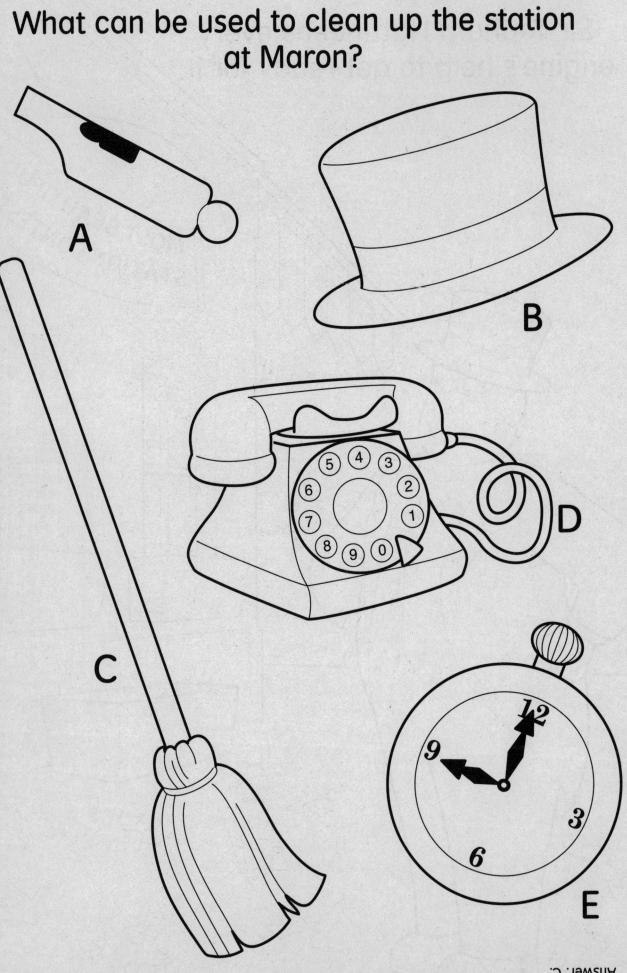

A

B

C

D

E

Thomas goes to the country to pick up a surprise for the contest. What does he see on his trip?

Thomas sees his friend Bertie, too!

Who is everyone waiting for?

"Percy, can you find something to
make the station look special?"
asks Sir Topham Hatt.

"Oh, no!" cries Percy. "I don't know what to bring."

Achoo! Percy thinks of something to bring to the station. What is it?

"My delivery will make the station smell fresh and sweet," cheers Percy.

Harold wants to help, too! What is he bringing to the station?

"Glad you made it, Harold,"
says Sir Topham Hatt.
"We need to start cleaning!"

Gordon is picking up some helpers to bring back to the station.

What are they bringing to help the station look as good as new?

James is picking up some special decorations.

What are they?

Everyone is working hard to get the station ready.

You can help fix up the station, too!

Percy's delivery adds the final touch!

Can you add some spring flowers to the station?

The stationmaster has something special
to add, too. Help him decorate.

Oh, no! A spring shower surprises everyone. Can you help Sir Topham Hatt find his umbrella? Circle it!

"I hope the rain doesn't ruin all our hard work," says Sir Topham Hatt.

The rain is stopping, and the contest judges will be here soon, but Thomas is running late!

Thomas unloads the surprise delivery just in time. What is it?

Finally, the station is ready.

The judges choose a winner!

Thanks to Thomas and his friends, Maron Station wins the contest!

THE MOST BEAUTIFUL STATION WINNER